To renew, find us online at:
https://capitadiscovery.co.uk/bromley
Please note: Items from the adult library may also
accrue overdue charges when borrowed on
children's tickets.

In partnership with

BETTER

For Rupert, Charlotte,
Michael and Joanna M.B-H.
For Lisa and Alfredo F. P.

林 拔 芙 華 人 協 會

LAMBETH CHINESE COMMUNITY ASSOCIATION

Special thanks to Jessie Lim at the LCCA
for her advice and guidance.
LCCA's Arts & Festivals Project promotes
Chinese culture and encourages community
participation in a range of art forms including
writing, visual arts, storytelling and drama.

Copyright © 1998 Zero to Ten Ltd
Text copyright © 1996 Margaret Bateson-Hill
Illustrations copyright © 1996 Francesca Pelizzoli

Edited by Anna McQuinn • Designed by Sarah Godwin
Screen-printing by Suzy McGrath

First published in the United States in 1996
by DeAgostini Editions.
This edition published in 1998
by Zero to Ten Ltd and distributed by
Laroussse Kingfisher Chambers
95 Madison Avenue, New York, New York 10016

Hardcover ISBN 1-84089 035-5
Paperback ISBN 1-84089 011-8

Library of Congress Cataloging-in-Publication Data
applied for.

Printed and bound in Italy

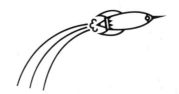

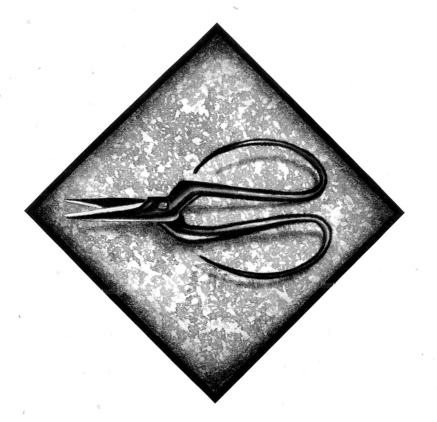

By **MARGARET BATESON-HILL**

Illustrated by
FRANCESCA PELIZZOLI

Chinese text by
MANYEE WAN

Paper cuts by
SHA-LIU QU

Lao ∗ Lao
of Dragon Mountain

很久以前，中國有一位老婆婆，人人都叫她做姥姥。她住在龍山腳下的一個小村莊裡。龍山上，住着一條冰龍。✴ 姥姥的屋旁有一塊園圃。她在那種着菜，過着簡單愉快的生活。✴ 她從來不會感到寂莫；因為她最喜歡坐在屋子外面，四周圍着村裡來的孩子們。在那兒，她從口袋裡拿出一塊薄薄的紙和一把小小的剪刀，一邊剪，一邊唱：『折一折，剪一剪，翻一翻，打開它，看一看，什麼最相像。』

LONG AGO in the country of China there lived an old woman.

She was known to everyone as Lao Lao and she lived in a tiny village which lay cradled in the foothills of Lung Shan – the mountain where the Ice Dragon reigned.

She led a simple and happy life, growing vegetables in the small garden next to her house. She was never lonely, for her greatest pleasure was to sit outside her home surrounded by the children of the village.

There she would take a thin sheet of paper and the small pair of scissors that she kept in her front pocket, and while she cut she sang,

Fold it and cut it and turn it around
Open it up and see what you've found.

NOW, so beautiful and delicate were these paper cuts that the fame of the old woman spread. People from the towns started to climb up the steep, narrow path to ask Lao Lao for one of her paper cuts.

They would always find her sitting outside her house, busy with her scissors and singing,

> *Fold it and cut it and turn it around*
> *Open it up and see what you've found.*

And the children would watch in amazement as she unfolded the piece of paper – what would it be? A butterfly! A rooster! A flower!

There would always be something for everyone, and Lao Lao would watch the children running home, each holding their own special gift. And as they ran, she would hear them singing,

> *Fold it and cut it and turn it around*
> *Open it up and see what you've found.*

姥姥美麗精巧的剪紙，很快便把她的名氣傳揚開去了。❋城裡的人們
開始爬上了斜斜的山坡、走上了窄窄的小路，來向她要剪紙。❋他們
經常會看到她坐在屋子外，忙碌地剪着，唱着：『折一折，剪一剪，
翻一翻，打開它，看一看，什麼最相像。』❋小孩子們一邊好奇地看着
她將紙打開，一邊猜：這次會是什麼呢？一只公雞！一朵花！一只蝴
蝶！❋沒有人會空手而回呢！姥姥喜歡看着孩子們手中拿着他們的特別
禮物，快快活活地一邊跑回家，一邊唱：『折一折，剪一剪，翻一
翻，打開它，看一看，什麼最相像。』

NOT very far from Lung Shan was the court of the emperor of all China.

One day a young serving maid received a paper flower from one of her relatives in Lao Lao's village.

The news spread throughout the palace.

"Oh, the color."

"Oh, it's so delicate, so beautiful – like a real flower."

"Yes," said the excited girl, flattered to be the center of so much attention, "they say she can make anything!"

THE emperor was a man of
great power and wealth, but
he was also cruel and greedy.
  Seated high upon his throne,
he overheard their chatter and
his eyes burned with desire.
  "Anything," he thought,
"she can make anything…"

離龍山不遠處，是大中
國皇帝的宮殿。＊一天，宮
中一名侍女從她住在姥姥村
裡的親戚處得了一朵紙花。
整個皇宮都在談論着它。
＊『啊，那顏色！』『啊，
多精巧！』『真美，像一朵
真的花一樣！』『是呀，』
侍女興奮地說，為引起了這
麼多人的注意而感到高興，
『聽說她什麼都會做呢！』

這個中國皇帝很有權勢
和財富，但他也很是殘暴
和貪心。＊皇帝坐在高高
的寶座上。聽見了宮中的
對話，他的眼睛發出貪婪
的光茫。『什麼都會，』他
想着，『她什麼都會做…』

THE emperor went to a secret room at the top of the palace. He always went there when he needed to think.

He paced up and down, lost in thought. Finally, he stopped in front of the window.

In the far distance he could see the mountain in whose shadow the old woman lived. A smile of satisfaction slowly spread across his face.

He immediately summoned two of his most trusted guards. Minutes later they were seen riding from the palace in the direction of the mountain.

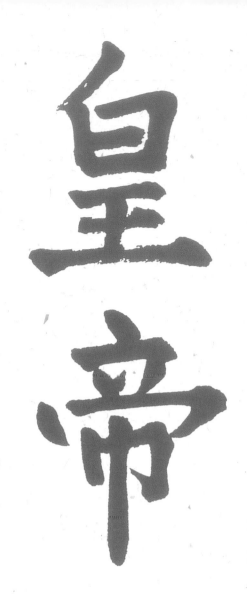

皇帝走到宮內最高頂樓上的一個密室裡。他每次有事情要想的時候，總會到這裡來的。✱他在室內踱來踱去，沉思著，最後停在窗子前。✱望向遠處，他可以看到老婆婆居住那座山的影子。一個滿足的笑容，慢慢從他的面上浮上來。✱他立即宣召來二名他最信任的衛兵。一會兒，便見衛兵離開皇宮，騎著馬向着龍山的方向跑去。

IT was the end of a long and tiring day for Lao Lao. The air was cold. There had hardly been any visitors.

She was getting ready for bed when suddenly she heard a noise from outside that made her afraid.

"OPEN UP!" came a harsh voice. "In the name of the emperor, open up or we'll break down your door!"

The old woman quickly opened the door as they asked, but the guards dragged her out into the night.

又是一個漫長疲倦的一天，這晚的空氣很是寒冷，人客也稀少。姥姥正準備上床休息，突然她聽到門外一個可怕的聲音：

『開門！』粗暴的聲音喊道。『皇上命你立刻開門，否則便要撞門了。』姥姥連忙把門打開，但馬上被外面的衛兵拖出黑暗中去。

UP the mountain they climbed
in the dark and the cold, until
the old woman thought she could
not go any further.

Then she found herself being
pushed up some steep stone steps.

ROUND and round, higher and
higher they climbed, until they came
to a door at the top of the tower.

The guards pulled away a large
iron bolt and the door creaked open.
Inside was a small room.

他們在黑暗與寒冷中往山上爬，直
至到老婆婆再也走不動了。然後，
她被推上一道陡峭的石級。

他們彎彎曲曲地向上爬，直至到了
一所塔樓頂上的一個小門前。衛兵
把門上的鐵栓拉開，門吖的一聲打
開。裡面是一個小小的房間。

THE room had only one small window. It was bare except for a chest, a small table with a lighted candle and a sharp pair of scissors. In the far corner was the largest pile of paper Lao Lao had ever seen.

"What does all this mean?" she managed to cry out. Her voice was thin and tired.

"The emperor has heard of your skill and commands you to make jewels for him," said the guard.

"Jewels – I don't know how to make jewels," cried the old woman, "I just take paper and cut simple shapes."

"The emperor has ordered you to fill the chest – so I suggest you start," said the other guard, harshly.

With that they turned and shut the door, locking it as they went. Lao Lao heard them climb down to the bottom of the tower.

房間裡有一個小小的窗戶，房內只有一個箱子和一張小桌子。桌子上擺着一支點燃的蠟燭和一把鋒利的剪刀。遠處的角落，堆著一堆姥姥從未見過那麼多的紙。＊『這是什麼意思？』姥姥喊道。她的聲音細弱和疲倦。

＊『皇上聽說了你的本領，現在要你給他造一滿箱的珠寶。』衛兵說。＊『珠寶？我不會造珠寶，』姥姥叫道，『我只會剪剪一些簡單的紙玩意兒。』＊『皇上命令你把這寶箱子裝得滿滿的，你還是快點動工吧。』衛兵說完了便鎖上門離去。姥姥聽着他們的腳步聲走到塔樓下。

姥姥看了看房子的周圍；好冷呵！這裡並沒有暖氣，唯一的燈光就是桌子上點燃的蠟燭。她怎麼辦啊？＊看來，答案只有一個。她走到那堆紙前，驚訝地看着，她從未見過那麼精美的紙啊！又滑又薄，每一張都是耀眼的純白色。『是要鑽石吧…』老婆婆想。她開始動手了。拿起那小剪刀，可能是習慣，又可能是給自己打氣，她開始唱着：『折一折，剪一剪，翻一翻…』＊但，她的聲音顫抖着，兩行淚珠沿着臉慢慢流下。她感到很孤獨，因為沒有孩子們在身邊看她剪紙。『當作孩子們都在這吧，』她輕輕的對自己說。

LAO LAO looked around the room and sighed. It was cold. There was no fire and the only light came from the candle on the table. What was she to do?

There seemed to be only one answer. She went over to the paper and looked in amazement. She had never seen such fine paper before – so smooth and thin, each piece a pure but dazzling white.

"Diamonds, I suppose," said the old woman. She set to work, taking the small sharp scissors laid out for her, and, perhaps from habit, or perhaps to give herself courage, she started to sing,

Fold it and cut it and turn it around...

But her voice faltered and two tears fell slowly down her face. She felt so alone, with no children there to watch her cut the paper.

"Perhaps if I pretend they are here..." she whispered.

折

一折、剪一剪

LAO LAO worked hard. Piece after piece she folded and cut, and the treasure chest started to fill up with the pieces of carefully cut paper.

   As it came to the deepest and darkest part of the night, Lao Lao grew colder and colder. Her movements grew slower and eventually stopped. The clear black sky sparkled with diamonds of its own and a slip of cold moon shone in through the tower window, gently lighting the old woman's face as she lay exhausted on the stone floor with the cold freezing her bones.

姥姥不停地一塊又一塊
的折著，剪著。珠寶箱
子不停地裝入一片片精
巧的剪紙。＊但當夜漸漸
入深的時候，姥姥覺得
越來越冷了。她的動作
也越來越緩慢。最後，
她不能再繼續下去了。
她虛弱地躺在石板地
上，感覺到身體陣陣冰
冷。＊外面漆黑的天空中
閃爍著大自然的寶石，
一絲冷冷的月色從塔樓
的窗戶射進來，輕輕地
照在她的臉上。

塔樓下面，兩個衛兵正
在等待著，他們的旁邊
生著一堆火。

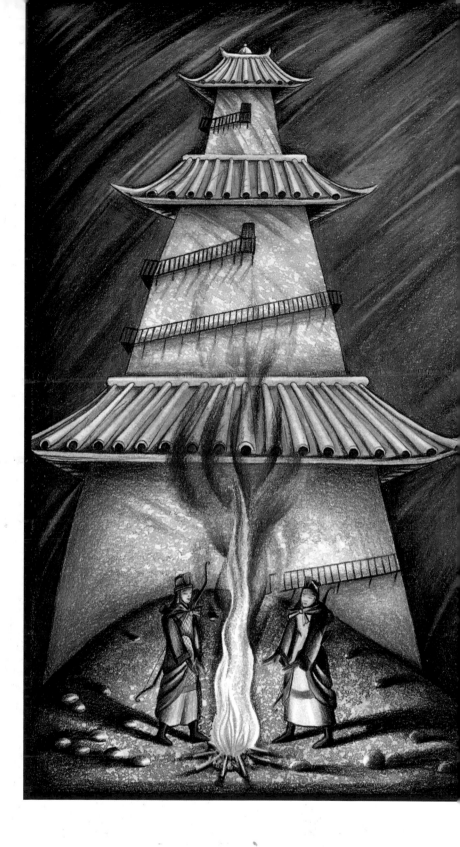

DOWN below, at the bottom of
the tower, stood the two guards,
waiting, and warming themselves
by a fire.

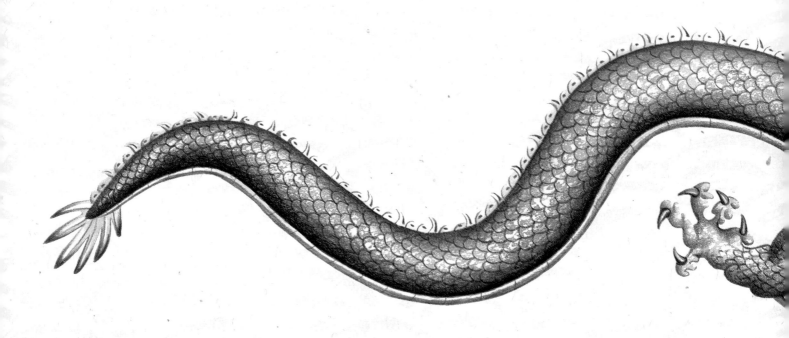

AND yet in all the darkness and stillness something was watching, something had seen everything – always saw everything – the Ice Dragon who slept at the top of the mountain.

Tonight the dragon knew that something was wrong…
He stretched forth his giant scaled body and, leaving his bed of snow, he flew over the land.

Below him lay tiny villages tucked in for the night and sprawling towns filled with busy people who had little time for rest.

He flew over the great palace of the emperor, then, circling back towards the mountain, he saw the emperor riding towards the tower.

然而，在這個黑暗與寂靜當中，一樣東西正在看着，牠什麼都看到了；牠什麼都看得見。牠—正是那頭躺睡在山頂上的冰龍。✳今天晚上，冰龍知道有事發生了。他伸展着那龐大的身軀，離開牠的雪床着大地飛去。地面上，小小的村落正籠罩在睡意中；懶洋洋的市鎮，住著每天為生活勞碌奔波的人們。✳冰龍飛越過皇帝的宮殿，跟着繞回山上。牠看見皇帝正騎著馬向塔樓走去。

ROUND and round the tower the Ice Dragon circled,
the anger rising in his chest as he saw the old woman lying
helpless on the floor.

From deep within him came a cry – ice-cold breath streamed
from his nostrils and froze the blood of the guards at the bottom
of the tower. The emperor fell from his horse, dazed by the sound,
unable to move.

Then the Ice Dragon gently picked up the old woman, lifting
her up high into the sky, safe from the guards, the emperor and
all further pain.

Lao Lao's papers billowed round in the ice-cold air, and,
as they fell, they turned into snowflakes, shining and sparkling in
the moonlight…

And when people woke in the morning the ground was
covered in papery, white snow.

冰龍繞着塔樓轉呀轉，看見孤弱無助的老婆婆躺在地
上，心中激起了憤怒。＊冰龍從心底發出一聲怒吼，
鼻子呼出冰冷的氣息，凝固了塔樓下衛兵的
血液。皇帝 被這巨大的聲音嚇得從馬背上
摔下來，不能動彈。＊冰龍輕輕地把老
婆婆從地上提起，帶到高空中，遠離
了皇帝與衛兵和所有的痛苦。姥姥的
剪紙四周飄灑著。當紙片落下來的時候，
變成了一片片耀目的、燦爛的雪花，在月
色中閃爍。＊人們在第二天的清早起來時，地
上已蓋上了一層厚厚的，紙花似的白雪。

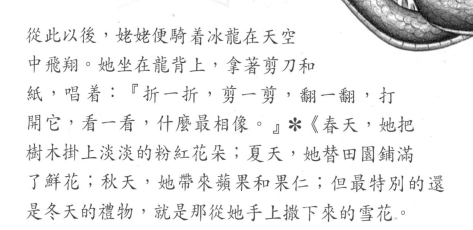

從此以後，姥姥便騎着冰龍在天空
中飛翔。她坐在龍背上，拿著剪刀和
紙，唱着：『折一折，剪一剪，翻一翻，打
開它，看一看，什麼最相像。』＊《春天，她把
樹木掛上淡淡的粉紅花朵；夏天，她替田園鋪滿
了鮮花；秋天，她帶來蘋果和果仁；但最特別的還
是冬天的禮物，就是那從她手上撒下來的雪花。

LAO LAO now rides on the back of the dragon. She flies all over
the land and whilst she sits, she takes a piece of paper and sings,

Fold it and cut it and turn it around
Open it up and see what you've found.

In spring she covers the trees with the palest of pink blossoms,
during the summer months the fields are filled with flowers,
and apples and nuts are her fall harvest. But, most special of all,
as a winter gift, white snowflakes drop from her hand.

THE tower on the mountain of the Ice Dragon is no longer standing. Instead you will find three pillars of ice. It is said that if you look very carefully, you can make out the figures of the emperor and his two guards. When they learn compassion, they will return to human form – but that is another story...

冰龍故事裡那座山的塔樓已經不在了。在山上，那兒現在可以看到三座冰柱。聽說，如果你仔細的看清楚，那原來是皇帝和他的兩個衛兵呢！不過，要是他們知道悔過的話，他們還是可以回復人形的—但，那已是另一個故事了。

THE END

CHINESE WRITING developed about 4,000 years ago. In the beginning, simple pictures stood for objects, words and ideas. Over a few hundred years, the picture signs were gradually simplified into the modern characters that are still used today. There are over 50,000 characters, but children can get by using a few thousand.

龍山姥姥
Lao Lao of Dragon Mountain

龍
Dragon

皇帝
Emperor

永
Forever

剪紙
Paper cutting

雪花
Snowflake

完
The End

MOUNTAIN

⌣
Old picture sign for **MOUNTAIN**

山
Modern character for **MOUNTAIN**

WOOD

木
Modern character for **WOOD**

林
Modern character for **FOREST**

MOUTH

口
MOUTH

欠
LIFT

吹
BLOW

China is a huge country and its inhabitants speak over 800 languages and dialects. However, because Chinese characters stand for ideas rather than sounds, Chinese people can all share the same writing system. Each Chinese character represents one idea and some words are made by putting two or more characters together. For example, "forest" is made from two "wood" characters and "blow" is made up of "mouth" and a character which means "to lift slightly."

IN CHINA, where paper was invented, people have been making paper cuts since AD 618. The art may have begun as a courtly pastime in the palaces of the great rulers, but today paper cutting is popular all over China.

At festival times, in China, and in places all over the world where Chinese people live, paper cuts are given as greetings or gifts and put on display.

The BUTTERFLY, FLOWER and SNOWFLAKE designs are symmetrical so, just like Lao Lao, you fold and cut them. You will need to use very thin paper.

The BUTTERFLY
is the simplest paper cut to make.

1 Take a piece of paper and fold it in half.
2 Copy or trace BUTTERFLY **A**.
3 Cut out the inside holes first, next cut around the edge, then open it up.

Fold Side

A

You can make a really pretty butterfly by using brightly patterned paper – wrapping paper works perfectly. Trace BUTTERFLY **A** onto tracing paper. Fold the patterned paper then staple the tracing paper to it. Cut through both the tracing paper and the patterned paper – inside holes first.

The FLOWER and SNOWFLAKE
are a little bit more complex.

1 Take a piece of paper 8½ in x 8½ in and cut it into a circle (**A**).

2 Fold it in half (**B**), then fold that into thirds (**C**) putting 1 in front and 3 behind so your piece of paper looks like the diagram (**D**).

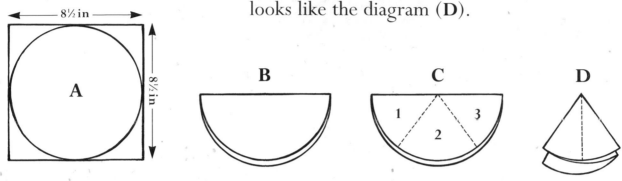

3 Then fold it in half one more time and trace the shape **E** or **F**.
Like the BUTTERFLY, staple the tracing to your paper.
Cut out the inside holes first, then go around the outer edge.
You could use a nice glittery paper for the SNOWFLAKE.

F
SNOWFLAKE

E
FLOWER

The DRAGON (next page)

is not symmetrical so you don't fold it. Instead, you simply trace the image from this book, staple the tracing paper onto colored paper and cut through both. Carefully cut the inside holes first (the staples will hold the papers together), then go around the edges.